D0819260

WELCOME TO
PASSPORT TO READING

A beginning reader's ticket to a brand-new world!

Every book in this program is designed to build read-along and read-alone skills, level by level, through engaging and enriching stories. As the reader turns each page, he or she will become more confident with new vocabulary, sight words, and comprehension.

These PASSPORT TO READING levels will help you choose the perfect book for every reader.

READING TOGETHER
Read short words in simple sentence structures together to begin a reader's journey.

READING OUT LOUD
Encourage developing readers to sound out words in more complex stories with simple vocabulary.

READING INDEPENDENTLY
Newly independent readers gain confidence reading more complex sentences with higher word counts.

READY TO READ MORE
Readers prepare for chapter books with fewer illustrations and longer paragraphs.

This book features sight words from the educator-supported Dolch Sight Word List. Readers will become more familiar with these commonly used vocabulary words, increasing reading speed and fluency.

For more information, please visit www.passporttoreadingbooks.com, where each reader can add stamps to a personalized passport while traveling through story after story!

Enjoy the journey!

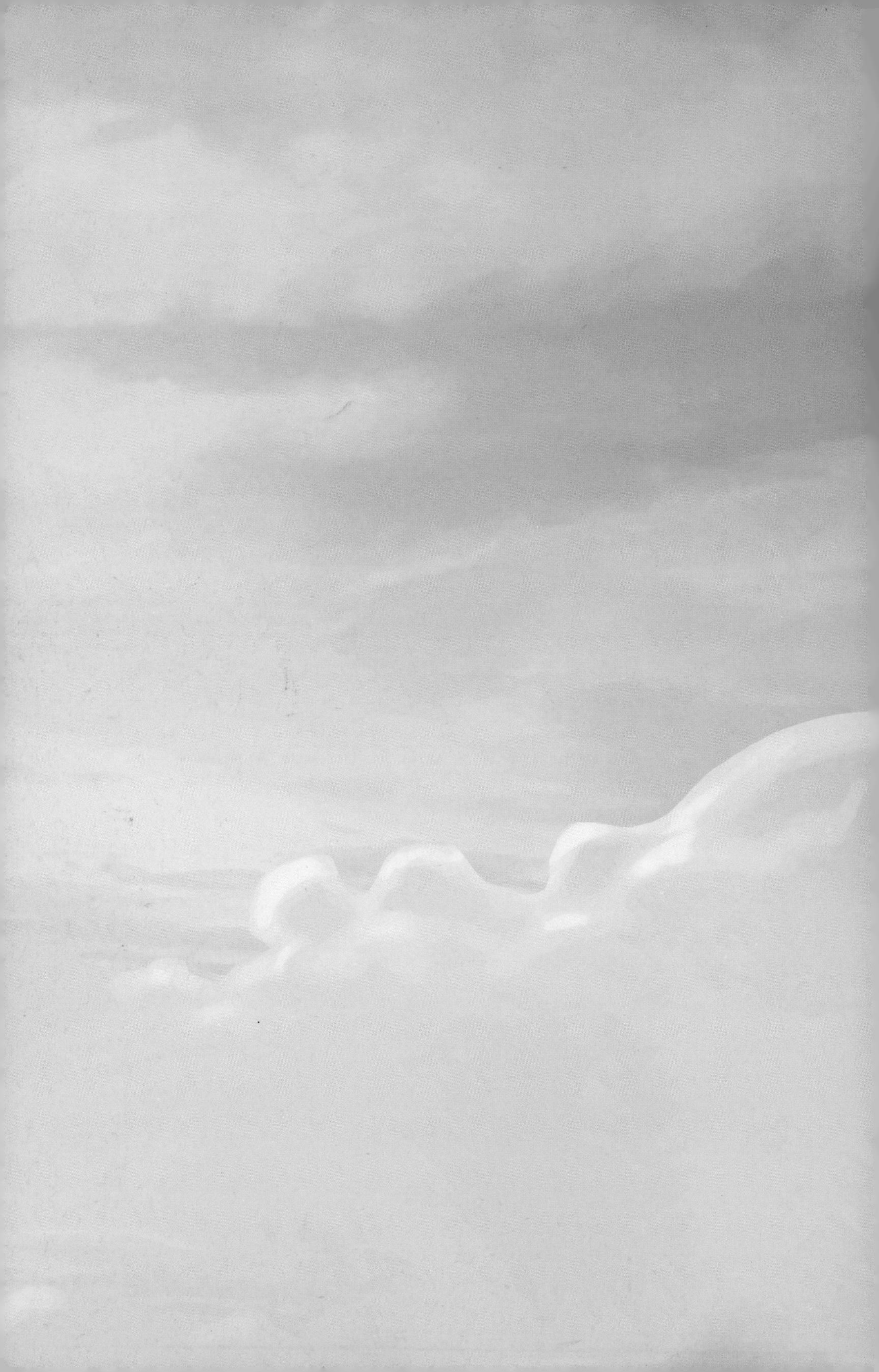

MARVEL
SUPER HERO SQUAD™

ADVENTURE COLLECTION

LITTLE, BROWN AND COMPANY
New York   Boston

marvelkids.com

Little, Brown and Company

Hachette Book Group
237 Park Avenue, New York, NY 10017
Visit our website at www.lb-kids.com

LB kids is an imprint of Little, Brown and Company.
The LB kids name and logo are trademarks of Hachette Book Group, Inc.

The publisher is not responsible for websites (or their content)
that are not owned by the publisher.

First Edition: August 2013

Team Spirit! originally published in September 2011
by Little, Brown and Company
The Trouble with Thor originally published in September 2011
by Little, Brown and Company
Meet the Villains of Villainville originally published in September 2010
by Little, Brown and Company
Super Hero Showdown! originally published in April 2012
by Little, Brown and Company
The Incredible Shrinking Squad! originally published in April 2012
by Little, Brown and Company

ISBN 978-0-316-22197-9

Library of Congress Control Number: 2012947191

10 9 8 7 6 5 4 3 2 1

LEO

Printed in China

Passport to Reading titles are leveled by independent reviewers applying the
standards developed by Irene Fountas and Gay Su Pinnell in *Matching Books
to Readers: Using Leveled Books in Guided Reading*, Heinemann, 1999.

MARVEL SUPER HERO SQUAD™

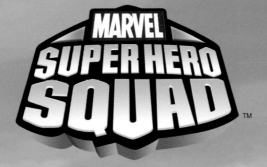

starring in

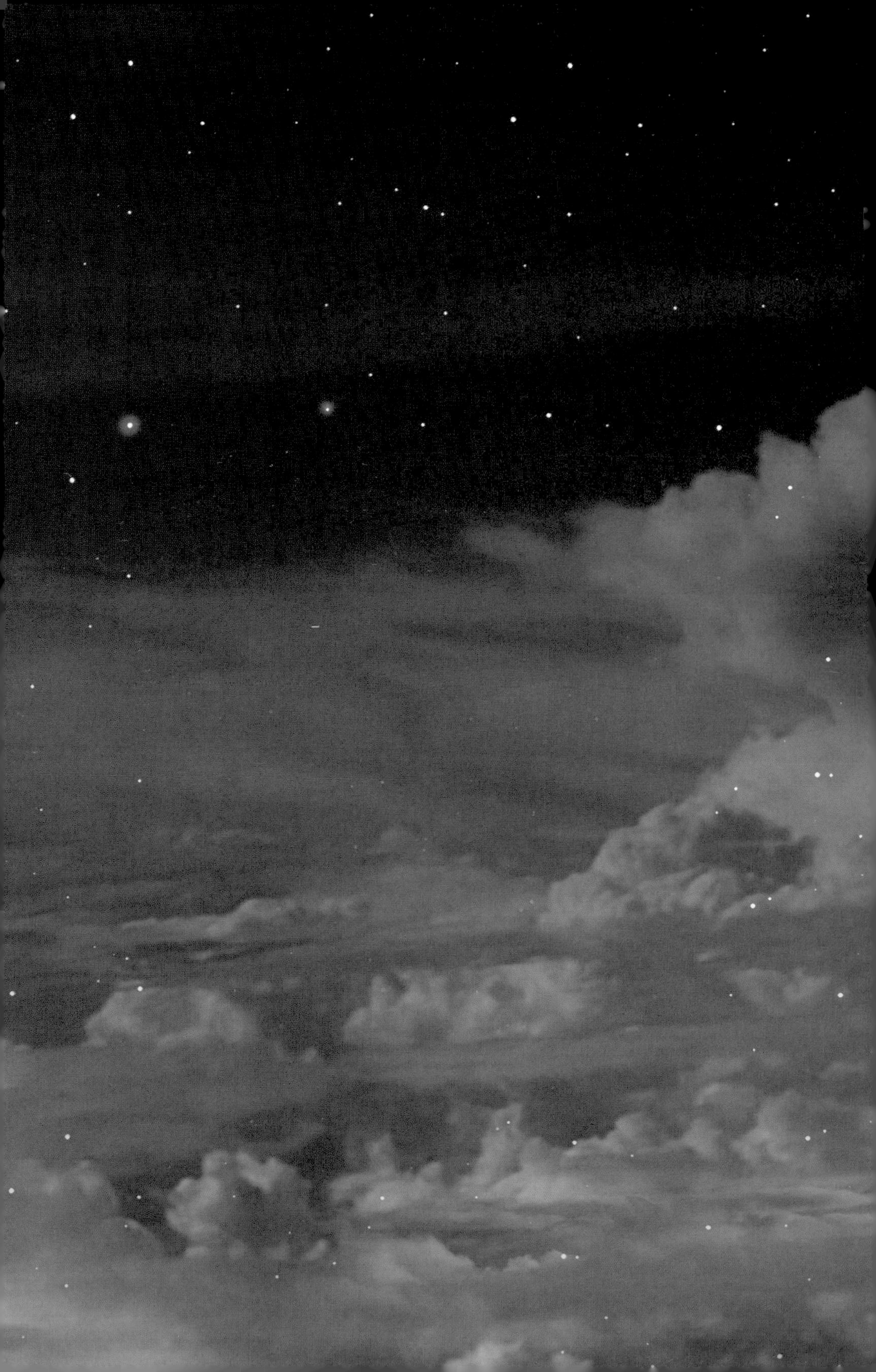

MARVEL
SUPER HERO
SQUAD™

TEAM SPIRIT!

by Lucy Rosen
illustrated by Dario Brizuela

LITTLE, BROWN AND COMPANY
New York   Boston

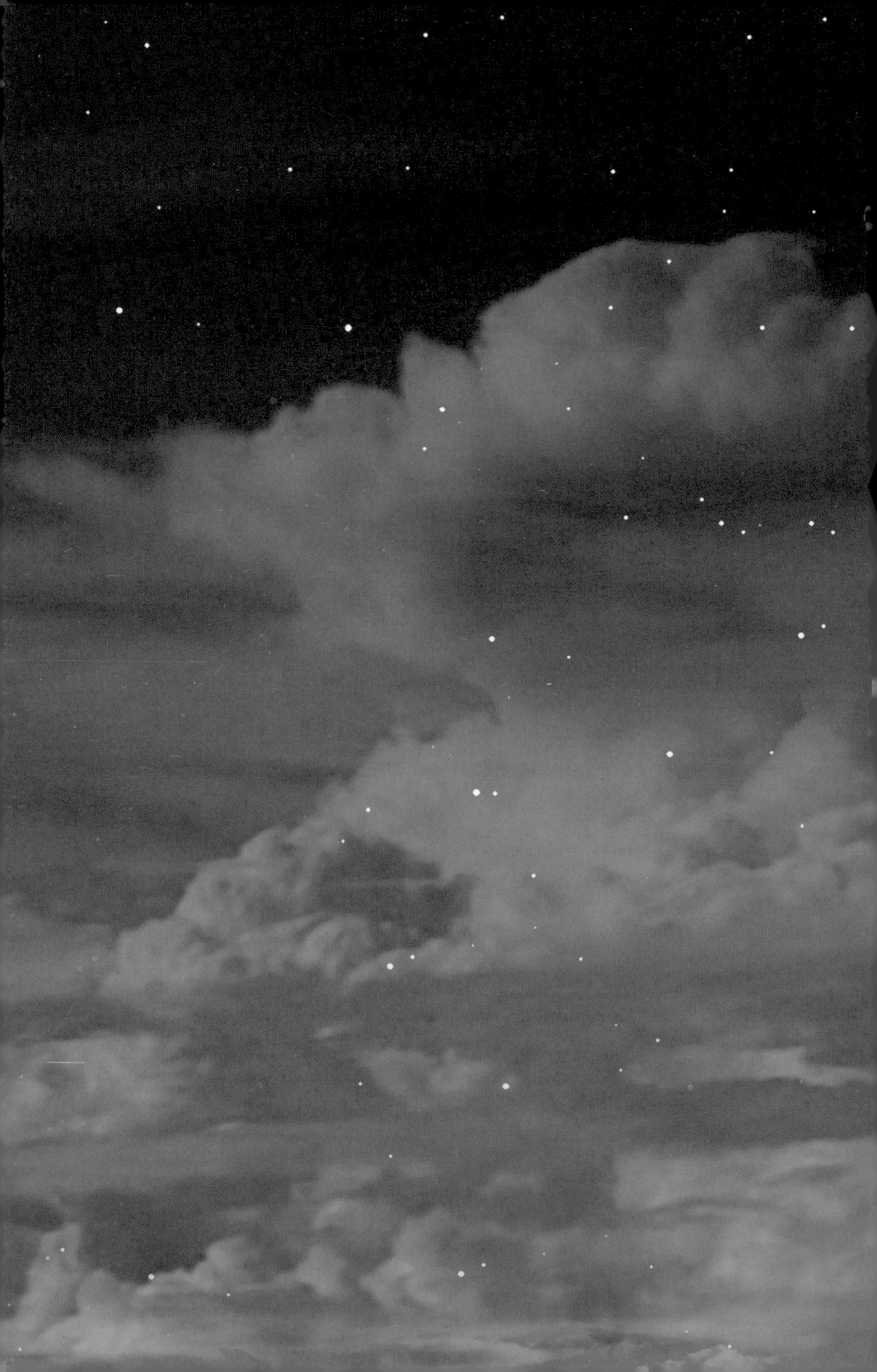

Attention,
all Super Hero Squad fans!

Look for these items when you read this story.

Can you spot them all?

SENTINEL

STATUE

WINGS

BIRD

Wolverine, Storm, and Spider-Man have just come back from a mission.

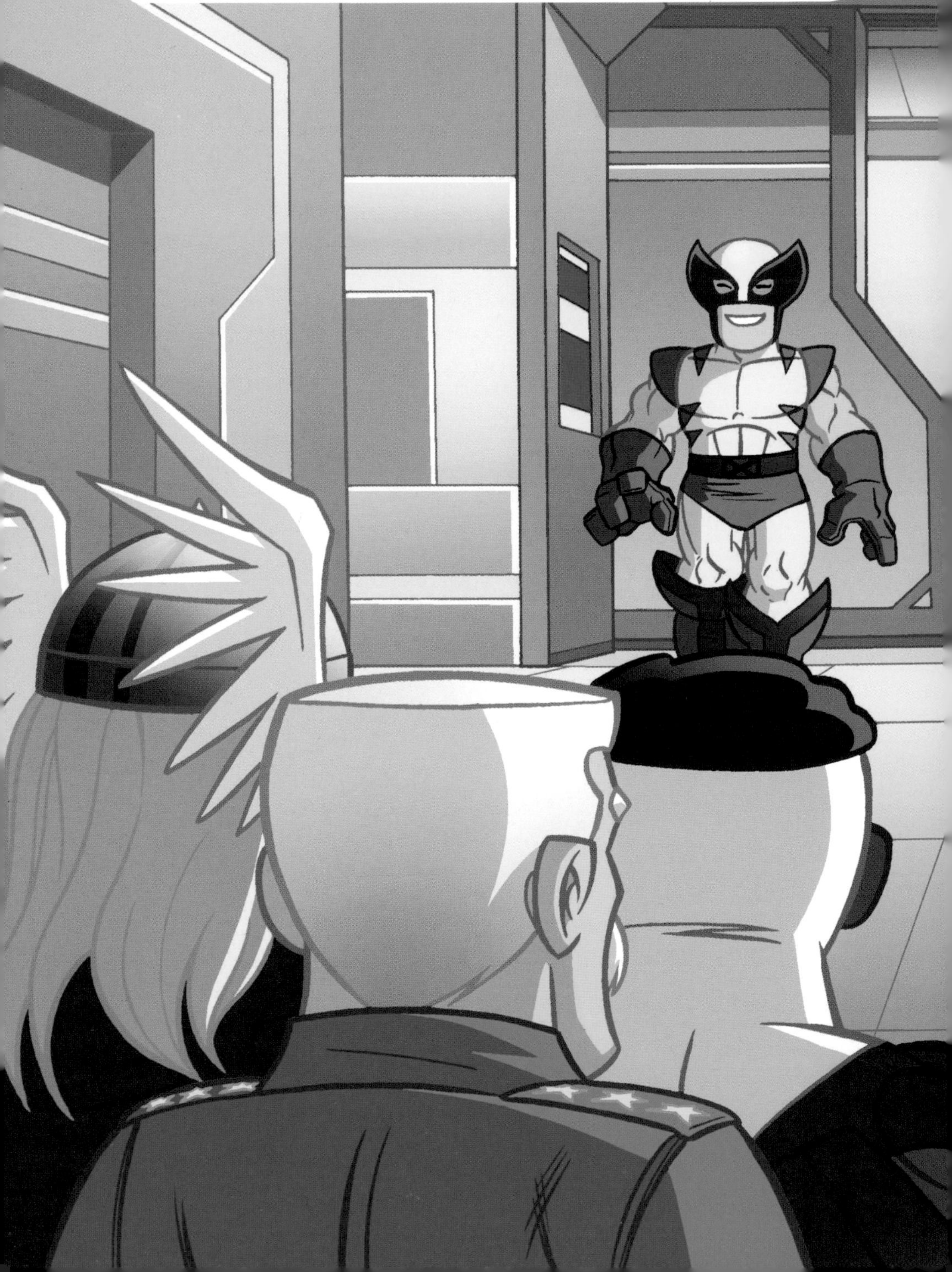

The Super Heroes want to tell
the rest of the Squad
about their big win.

"We hid in my fog cloud," says Storm, "to sneak into Dr. Doom's place. Spider-Man used his web to pull down the gate."

"Then Wolverine used his claws
to shut down the Sentinels.
The villains never even knew
we were there!"

"Wow," says Invisible Woman.
"That sounds…amazing."
"And a lot like their last three
amazing adventures," says Thing.

Wolverine hears what Thing and Invisible Woman say. He asks General Ross, "What do they mean?"

"You three do a great job," says Ross.
"But the other Squaddies
want to work with you, too."
"We like being a team," says Storm.
"We work so well together!"

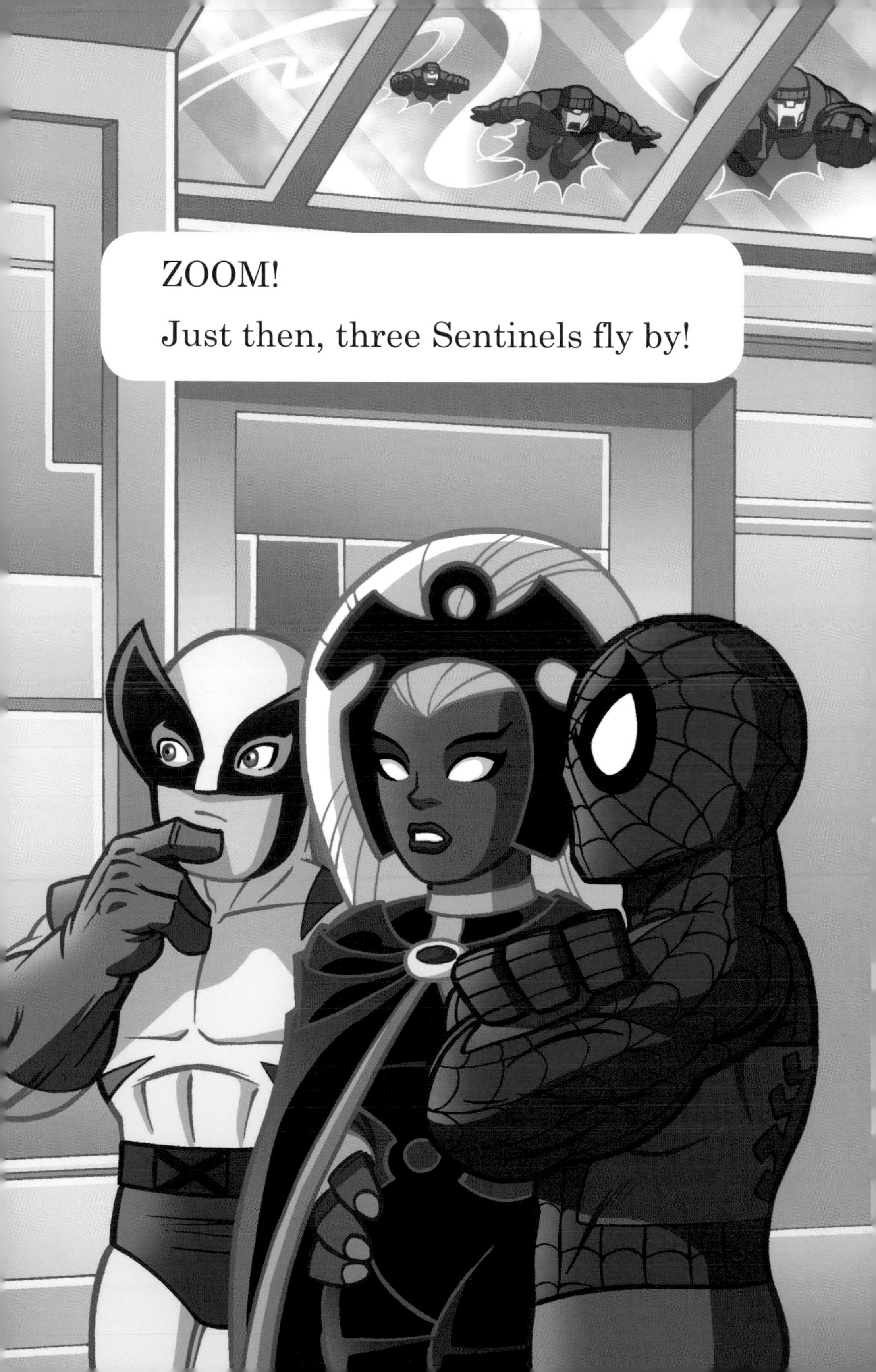

ZOOM!

Just then, three Sentinels fly by!

Dr. Doom appears on-screen.
"You cannot sneak into my lair
and get away with it!" he says, cackling.

"These Sentinels are going to three different places. You have ten minutes to find them before they destroy Super Hero City!"

"Squaddies, Hero Up!" cries General Ross. "Spider-Man, team up with Falcon. Wolverine, go with Invisible Woman. Storm and Thing, work together."

Wolverine, Spider-Man, and
Storm are not happy.
They want to work together.
But there is no time to argue.

Spider-Man tries to think of a plan.

"Where did the Sentinels go?" he asks.

"I do not know where to start!"

"I do," says Falcon.

Falcon asks his bird friends
to help look for the Sentinels.
The birds of Super Hero City
tell the two Squaddies to go to City Hall.

Falcon grabs Spider-Man
and jumps into the air.
The pair soar on Falcon's wings
and zoom over to City Hall.

"I spy a Sentinel!" says Spider-Man.

He uses a web to catch it.

The robot does not see the heroes coming.

"One down, two to go!" they cheer.

Wolverine and Invisible Woman

find a Sentinel at the bank.

The robot is climbing the wall.

"Hey, Sentinel!" cries Invisible Woman.

The Sentinel looks to its left,
and Invisible Woman disappears.
Then she reappears on the other side.
"I am right here!" she says, giggling.

As soon as the robot turns its head, Invisible Woman is gone again. The Sentinel gets so confused that it lets go of the wall!

The Sentinel crashes to the ground.
Wolverine leaps up to snip its wires.
"Nice job!" he says.
"Thanks!" says Invisible Woman.

There is one Sentinel still out there
and only two minutes left to find it!
Storm and Thing keep looking.
"We have to find it!" says Storm.

Suddenly, the Sentinel jumps out
from behind a building.
It starts running to attack at full speed.

"We need rain!" Thing calls out. Storm uses her powers to make drops of rain fall from the sky. A huge mud puddle forms.

The robot slips in the mud and falls.
Thing smashes his fist into a statue.
It crumbles down around the robot.
The Sentinel is trapped!

The Super Heroes tell General Ross how they defeated all three Sentinels. "Falcon was awesome," says Spider-Man. "So was Invisible Woman," says Wolverine. "So was Thing!" adds Storm.

General Ross winks.

"Sorry to break you up," he tells them.

"Do you want to be on one team again?"

Spider-Man, Storm, and Wolverine smile.
"We *are* on one team," they say,
gathering all their friends.
"We are on the Super Hero Squad!"

THE TROUBLE WITH THOR

by Lucy Rosen
illustrated by Dario Brizuela
inks by Andres Ponce

LITTLE, BROWN AND COMPANY
New York   Boston

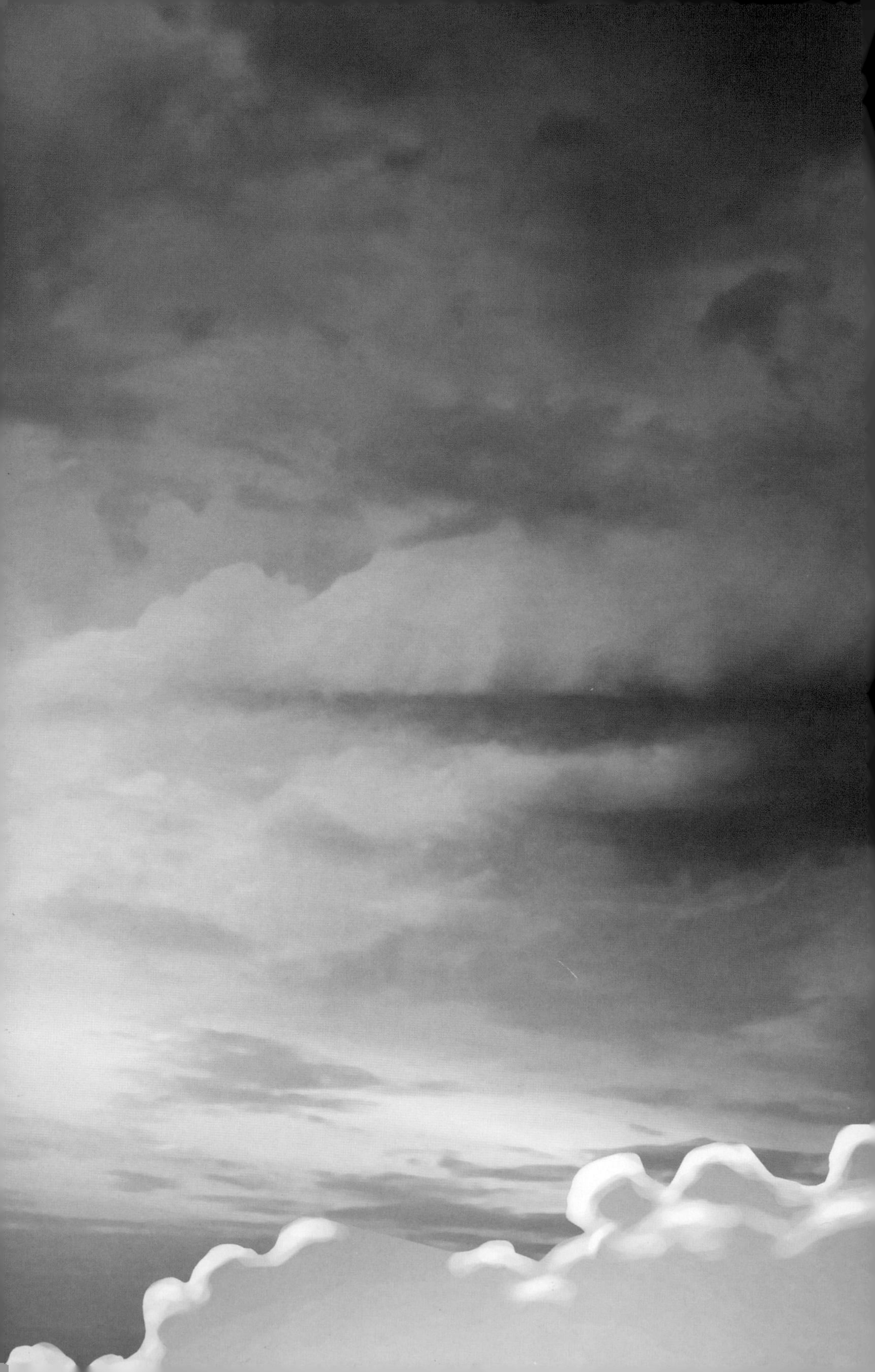

Attention,

all Super Hero Squad fans!

Look for these items when you read this story.

Can you spot them all?

SLIDE

POWER LINES

HAMMER

LIGHTNING BOLT

Thor wakes up one day
with a knot in his stomach.
"I have a bad feeling about today,"
he says with a shiver.

Thor tries to ignore his nerves.
He has to help the other Squaddies
build a new park in Super Hero City.
He needs to leave or he will be late.

On the way, Thor runs into someone he does not want to see.

"Loki!" Thor cries in dismay.

"What do you want?"

"Can't a villain visit his favorite half brother?" Loki asks with a smirk.

"I do not have time
for your tricks today," says Thor.
"Your powers are strong," says Loki.
"You belong in Villainville!"

"Never! Now beat it!" yells Thor.

"Fine," says Loki. "I will go.

But you know I am right!"

Loki's words scare Thor.

The knot in his stomach feels bigger.

Thor finally arrives at the park.

"There you are!" says Silver Surfer.

"We have a lot to do today.

Can you put this slide together?"

"No problem," says Thor.

He lifts his hammer and swings.

He swings too hard. BOOM!

The hammer smashes the slide!

"Are you okay?" asks Silver Surfer.

"I am fine," says Thor.

"I will fix that later.

What else can I do?"

"We need to fill the pool,"

says Dr. Strange.

"Can you make it rain just a little?"

Thor nods. That is easy.
He zaps the sky with his hammer
to make a small rain shower.
But the storm gets out of control.

It turns into a huge hailstorm!
Wind knocks over the power lines.
The Super Heroes run for cover!

"I am sorry!" yells Thor.

Thor stops the storm.

The park is in ruins.

He feels terrible.

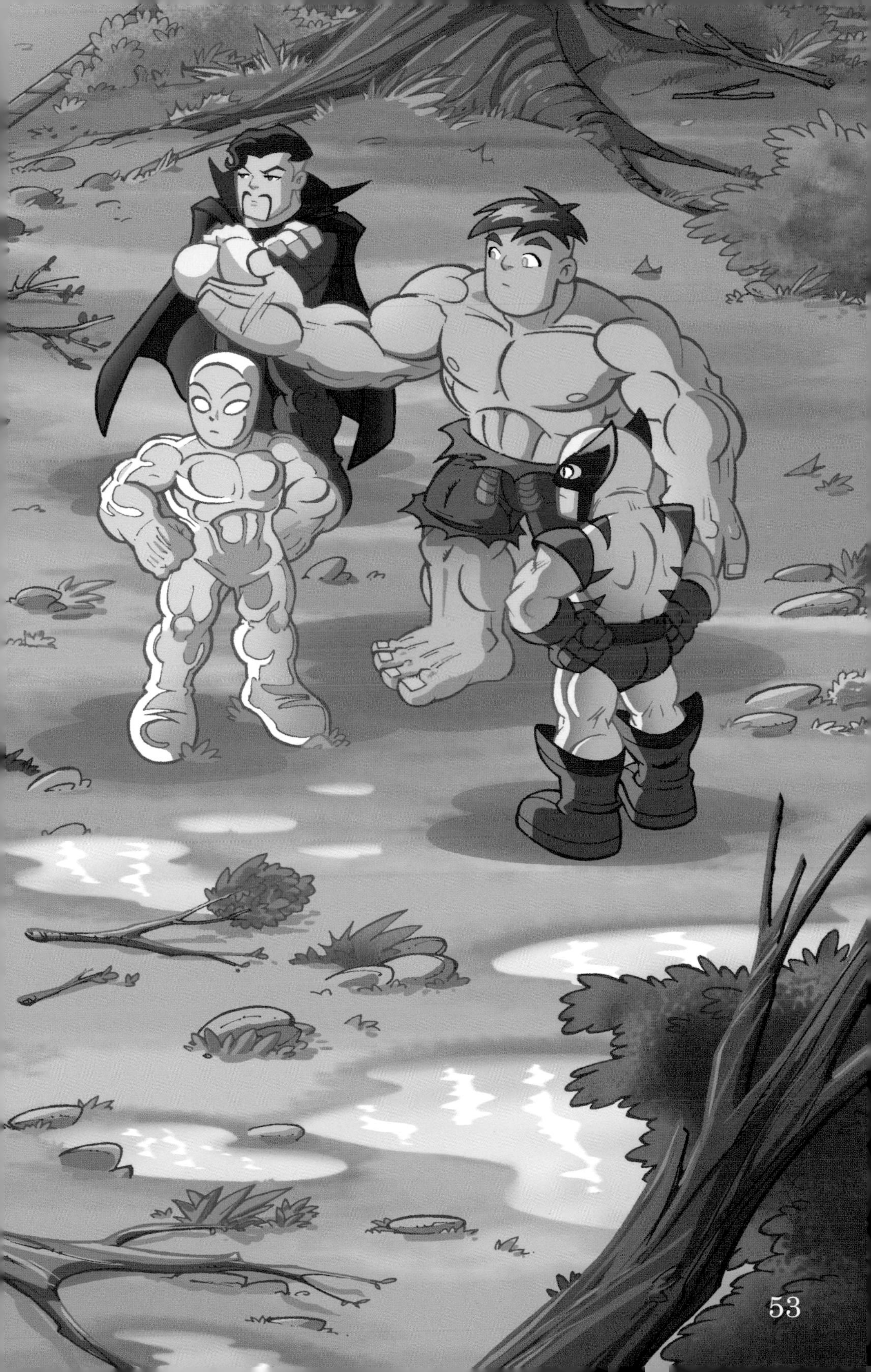

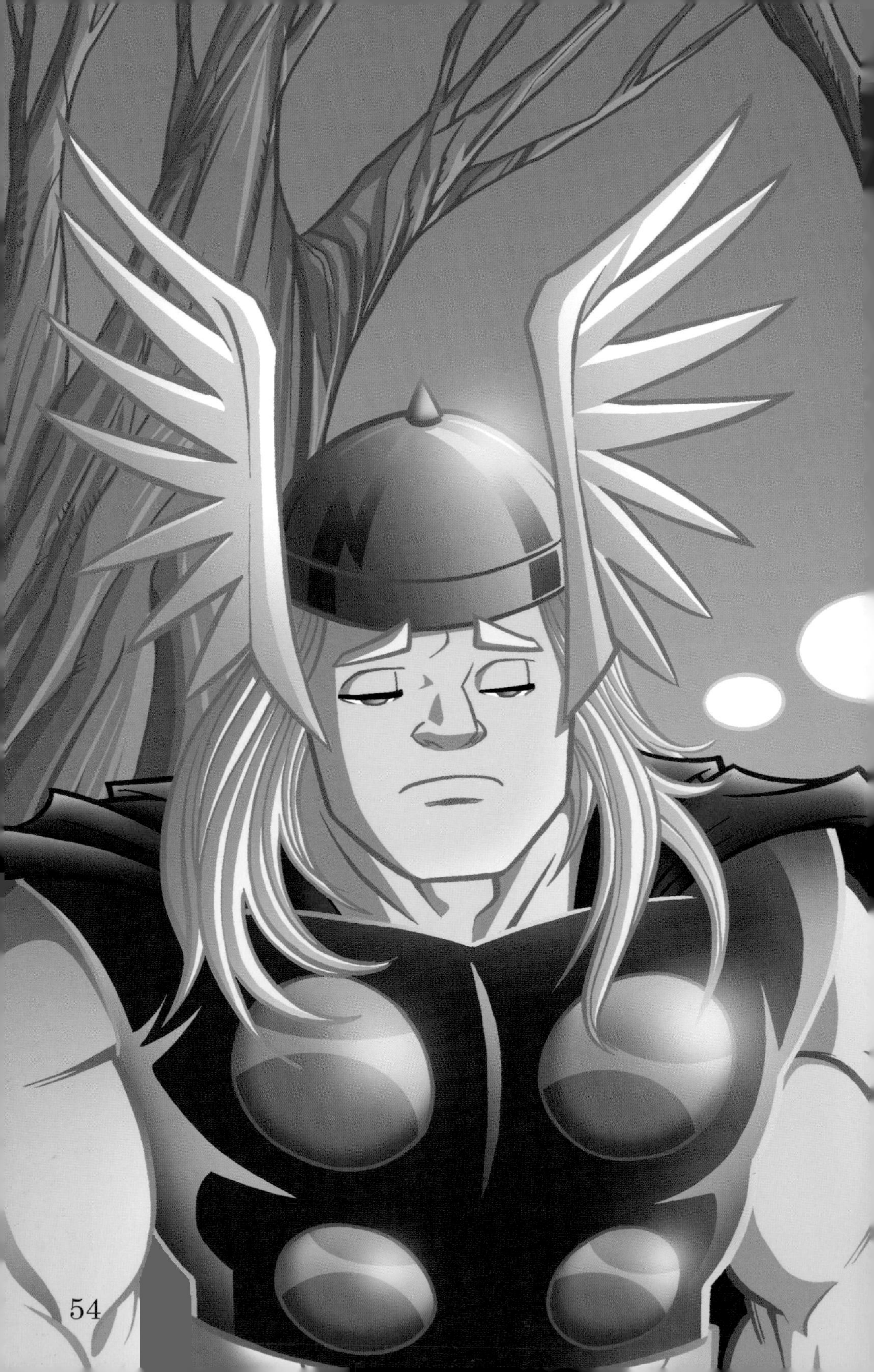

Thor does not know what to do.
Should he leave Super Hero City?
Should he go live in Villainville?

Back at Squad headquarters,
Thor hears an alarm.
"It's Magneto and Doc Ock!"
yells General Ross.
"They are attacking! We need you!"

"I ruin everything I touch today!"
Thor cries.
"I may not be able to help.
But I have to try anyway!"

Thor reaches the fight
as Magneto knocks Falcon down.
Doc Ock pins Iceman
with his long mechanical arms.

Things look bad
for the Super Hero Squad!

Thor's stomach tightens.

He worries he will mess up again,

but he has to try to help his friends!

He throws a lightning bolt at Doc Ock.

It shocks the villain's metal arms.

Doc Ock lets go of Iceman.

Thor makes rain, which rusts Doc Ock.

The villain cannot move his metal arms!

Magneto uses his magnetic force to drag Doc Ock behind him. He runs off, yelling to Thor, "You will never catch me!"

"I do not have to," says Thor.
He drops his hammer.
Magneto's power draws it
right to his own helmet!
The hammer knocks out the bad guy!

"You did it!" shouts the Squad.

"Thor saved the day!"

"No," argues Thor.

"I messed up the park today!"

"Even Super Heroes have bad days," says General Ross. "It did not stop you when we needed you most."

Thor smiles.

The knot in his stomach goes away.

He knows he is right where he belongs.

MEET THE VILLAINS OF VILLAINVILLE

by Lucy Rosen
illustrated by Dario Brizuela

LITTLE, BROWN AND COMPANY
New York   Boston

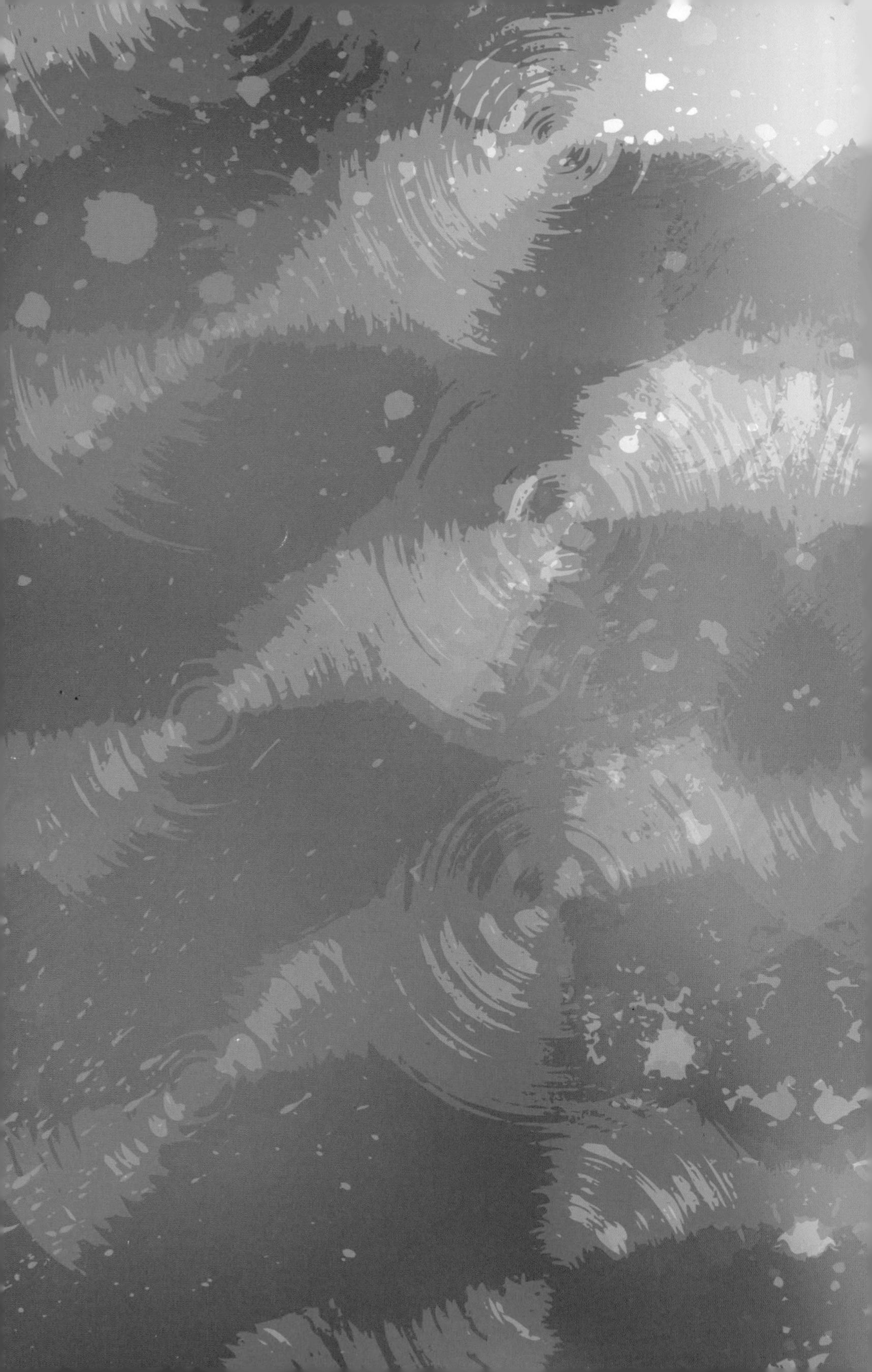

Attention,
all Super Hero Squad fans!
Look for these items when you read this story.
Can you guess which of your favorite
characters use them?

HELMET

IRON GLOVE

HORNS

HEADQUARTERS

The Super Hero Squad
protects Super Hero City,
watching over it from
the Squad's flying headquarters.

It is up to the Super Heroes
to keep their city safe from villains.

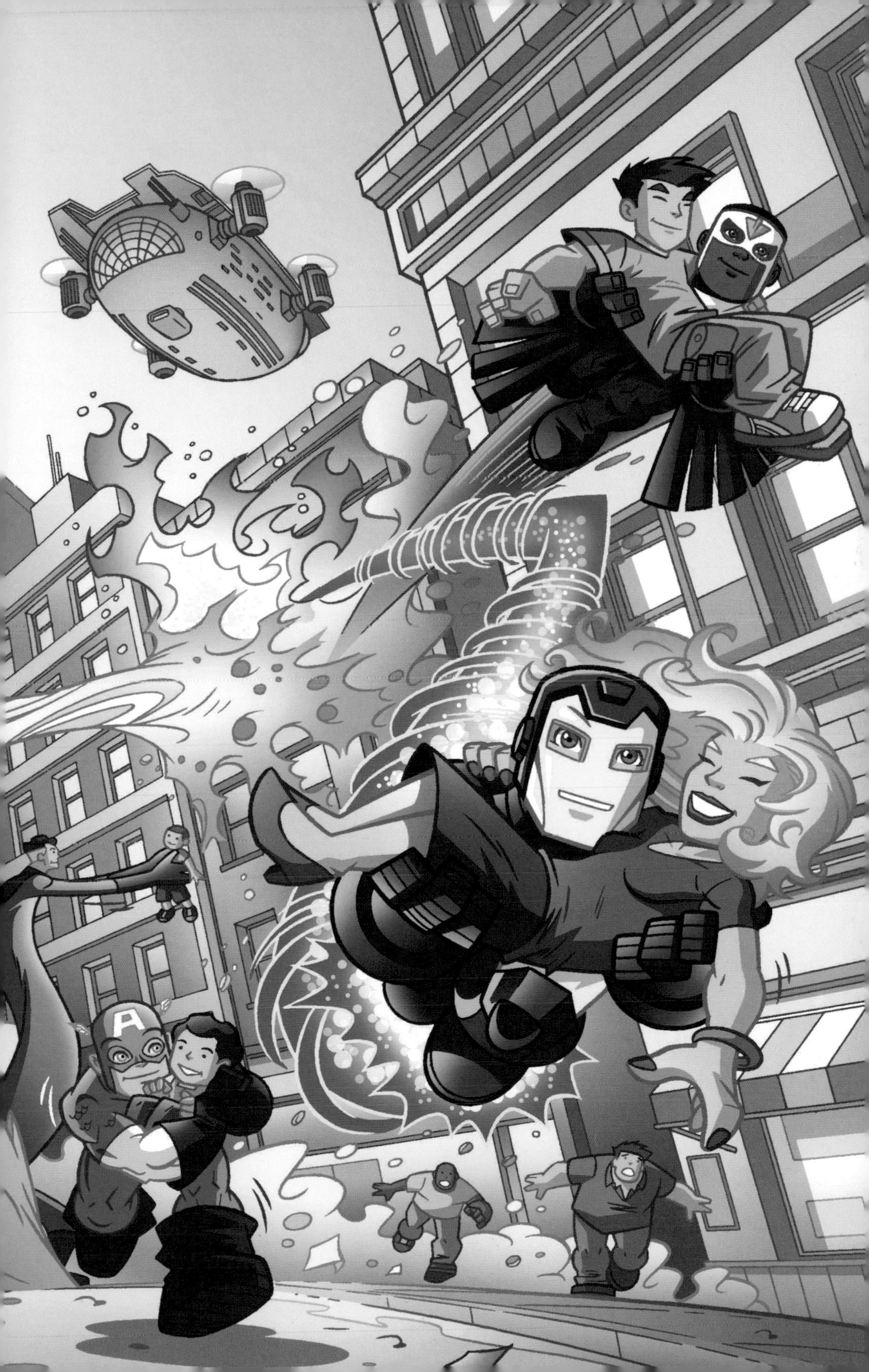

Across the river
from Super Hero City
is a dark and scary place.
It is called Villainville.

The skies are always stormy
in Villainville.
The homes need to be fixed,
and no one cares about the rules.

The bad guys who live in Villainville have one mission.

They want to make trouble
for all the heroes in
Super Hero City!

Dr. Doom is the leader
of this band of evildoers.
From his secret lair,
he gives the villains their orders.

He rules with an iron fist
and an army of robot Sentinels.
Now he wants to rule the world.
If only the Squaddies would
stay out of his way!

Magneto is the master of magnetism.

He can move anything made of metal.

But Magneto sometimes gets upset.
Metal objects can stick to him
when he does not want them!
Even superpowers can go wrong!

Super Skrull has many superpowers!
He can control fire,
generate force fields,
and become invisible.

He can also stretch superlong
and make his skin rock hard.
Skrull is like four villains in one!
He is Villainville's
most dangerous bad guy.

Loki creates mayhem wherever he goes. He plays magical pranks on all the Super Heroes.

Loki's favorite hero to annoy is his half brother, Thor!

Mystique likes to play
tricks of her own.

With skin that can change

size and shape,

this sly villain can be anyone's twin.

It makes her hard to catch!

Doc Ock's extra mechanical arms
make it easy for him to cause trouble.

The Super Heroes must be fast if they want to catch Doc Ock. He escapes by crawling away in no time!

Do not mess with Abomination!
He is one of the strongest guys around.

Abomination uses his mutated size to destroy everything in sight. He is Villainville's biggest bully.

When the Super Villains
need a little extra help,
they call on their army of robots.

The Sentinels can zoom through the air
and use cables to capture the heroes.
One thing is certain:
These fighting machines mean business!

The good guys in
Super Hero City
are brave, strong, and tough.

But these awful villains
are planning to give them a fight
the Super Heroes will not forget.

"Ready to attack the Super Hero Squad?" yells Dr. Doom to his gang of evil warriors.

"Ready!" scream the Super Villains.

This will be the biggest battle ever!

Who will win?

SUPER HERO SHOWDOWN!

by Lucy Rosen
illustrated by Dario Brizuela
inks by Andres Ponce • coloring by Franco Riesco

LITTLE, BROWN AND COMPANY
New York   Boston

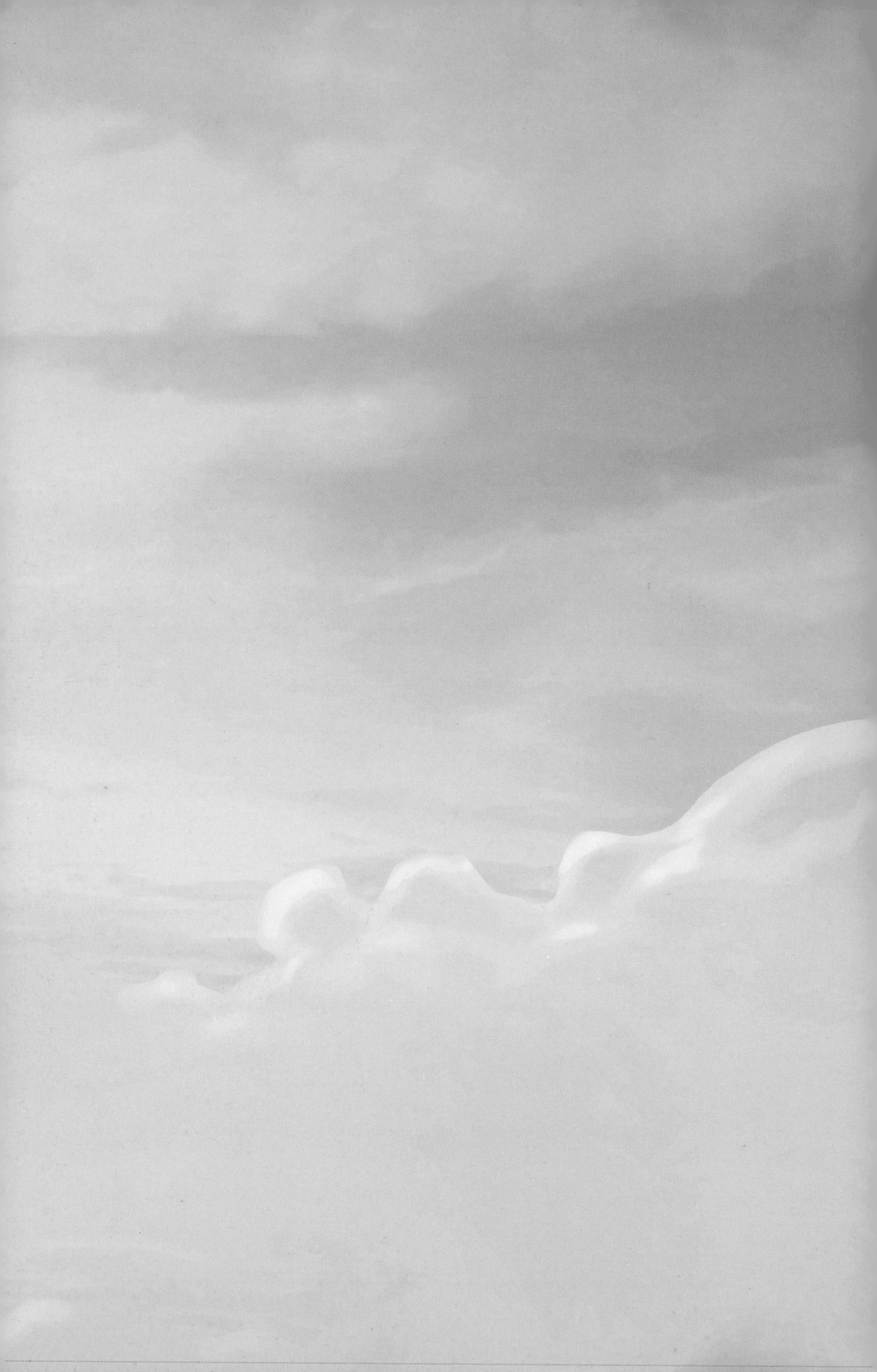

Attention,
all Super Hero Squad fans!
Look for these items when you read this story.
Can you spot them all?

JUGGERNAUT

MALLET

BOULDER

One warm afternoon,
the Super Hero Squad
goes to check out the city's
first summer carnival.

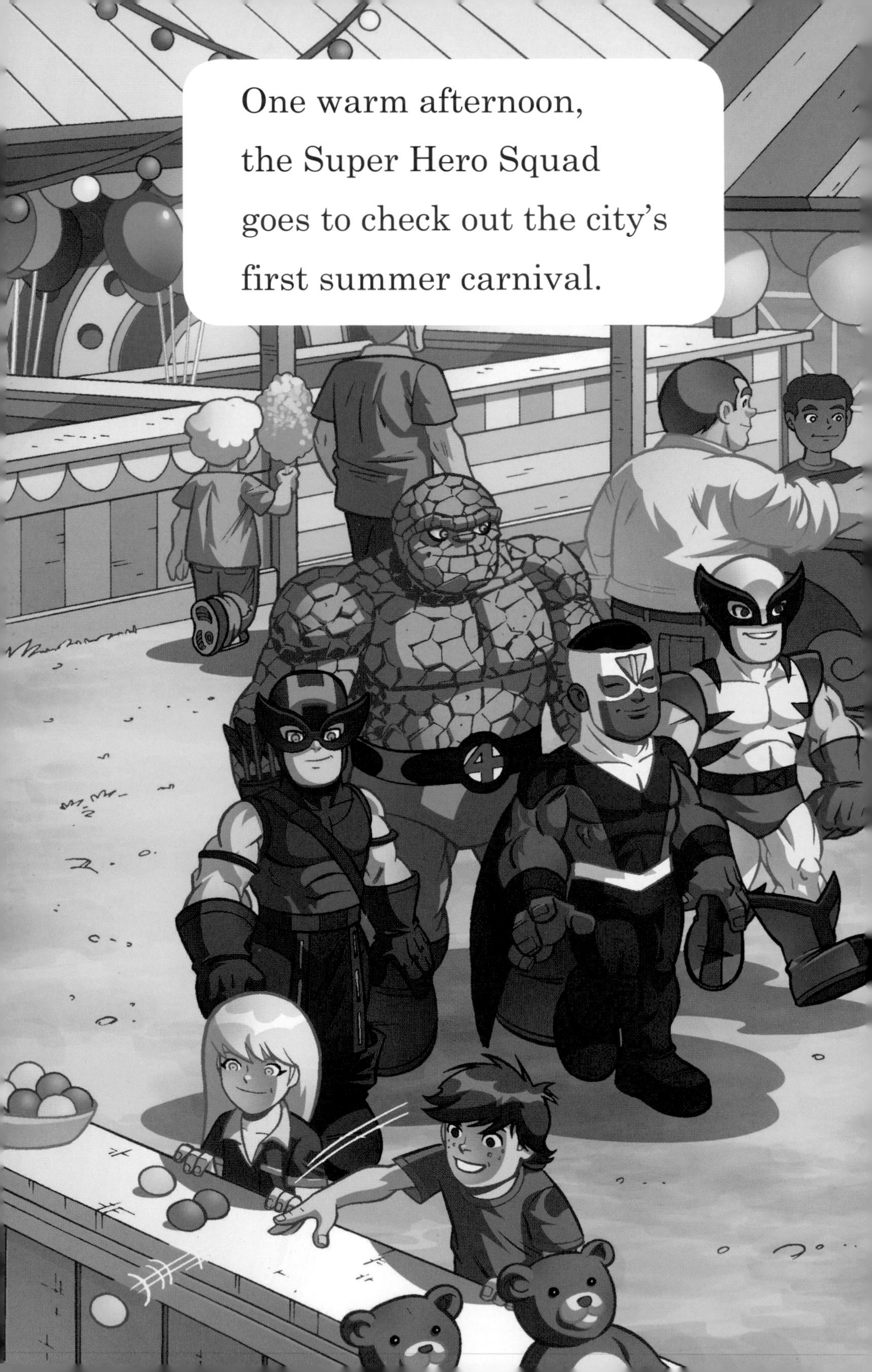

Luke Cage wants to try
the strength test.
"Step right up!" says Iron Man.
Luke takes the mallet.

"Piece of cake," brags Luke. "Strongman contests are kind of my thing!"

"I do not think so, Cage," someone growls.

It is Juggernaut!

"Let me show you
how it is done,"
says Juggernaut.
He grabs the mallet.
"I was first!" argues Luke.

"Be cool," says Iron Man.
"Today is about having fun."

105

Luke goes first.

He swings the mallet

as hard as he can.

DING!

Luke's hit rings the bell!

"Beat that," Luke says.
With one swift swing,
Juggernaut hits the bell, too!

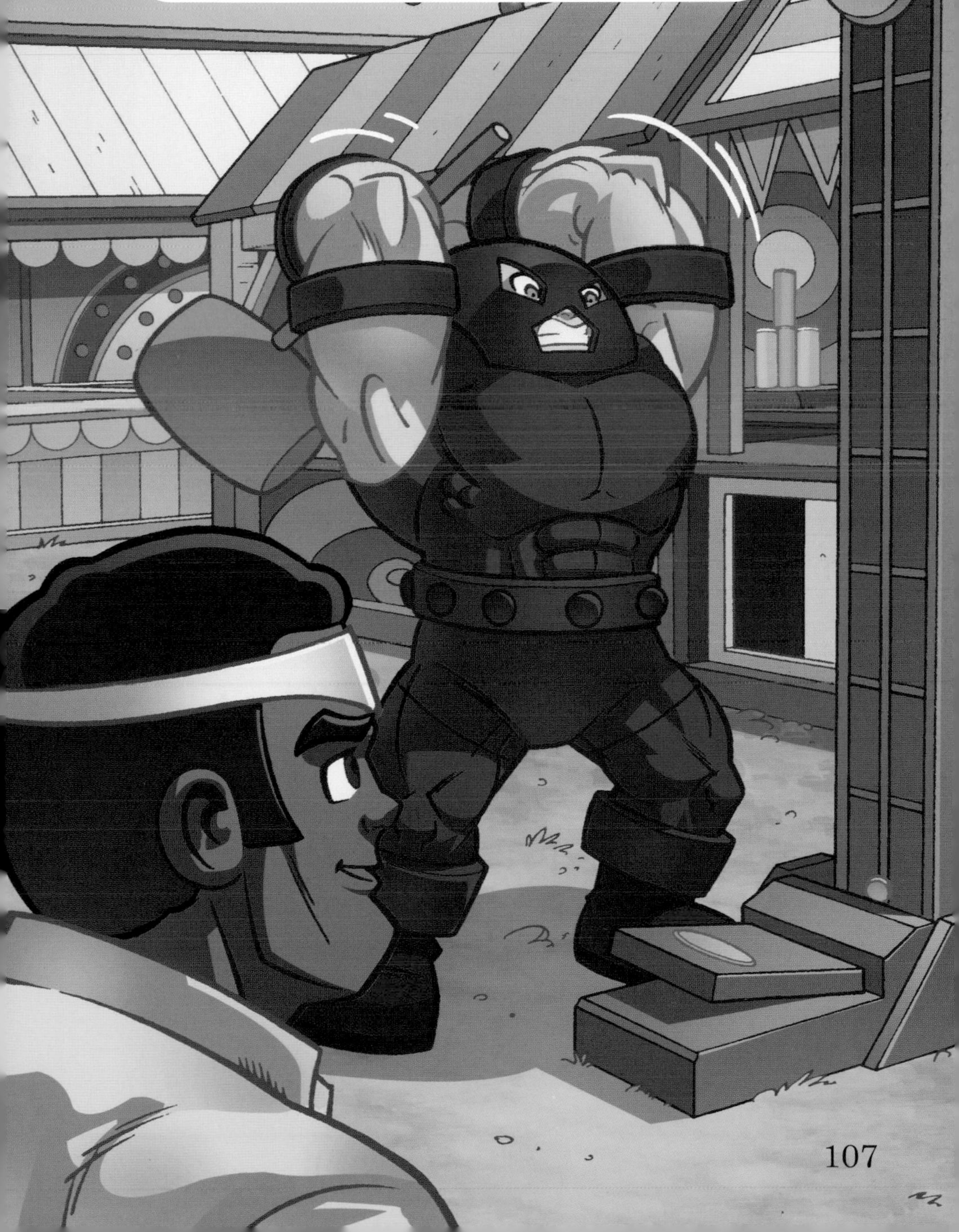

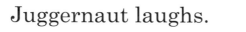

Juggernaut laughs.

"Now who is hot stuff?" he says.

"Anyone can get lucky," says Luke.
"Want to try another contest?
Best two out of three wins!"

The Squaddies are ready to help.

"Okay, guys," says Iron Man.

"First up, another strength test.

Who can lift the most?"

Juggernaut goes first.

He picks up a huge boulder.

"No sweat," he says.

"One rock? That is nothing," says Luke.

He walks over to his pal Thing.

In a flash, Luke lifts Thing

high above his head!

"This guy is like a mountain!" boasts Luke.

"That is true," laughs Iron Man.

"This round goes to Luke Cage!"

"Next up," says Iron Man,
"a climbing test!
Whoever climbs to the top
of the skyscraper first wins this one."

114

Falcon flies up to the roof.
"On your mark, get set, go!"
he shouts.

Juggernaut and Luke take off.

Luke gets a good start.

But suddenly, he cannot move.

His boot is stuck on a nail!

Juggernaut takes the lead.

Luke frees himself, but it is too late.

"Juggernaut wins!" cries Falcon.

The score is tied.

"Now you have to swim," says Iron Man.

"The first person to swim

across the river wins!"

Luke and Juggernaut
dive into the water.
Luke Cage pushes ahead.
He sees the other side
of the river getting closer and closer.

Luke looks back.

Juggernaut is far behind him.

I am going to win! Luke thinks.

Then he hears a cry. "Help!"
Luke treads water to listen.
He turns and sees a boy
splashing in the water.
The boy cannot swim!

Quickly, Luke swims
to the boy.
He pounds his arms and legs
to swim faster.

"Got you!" yells Luke
as he pulls the boy
onto his back.
Luke takes him safely
to the shore.

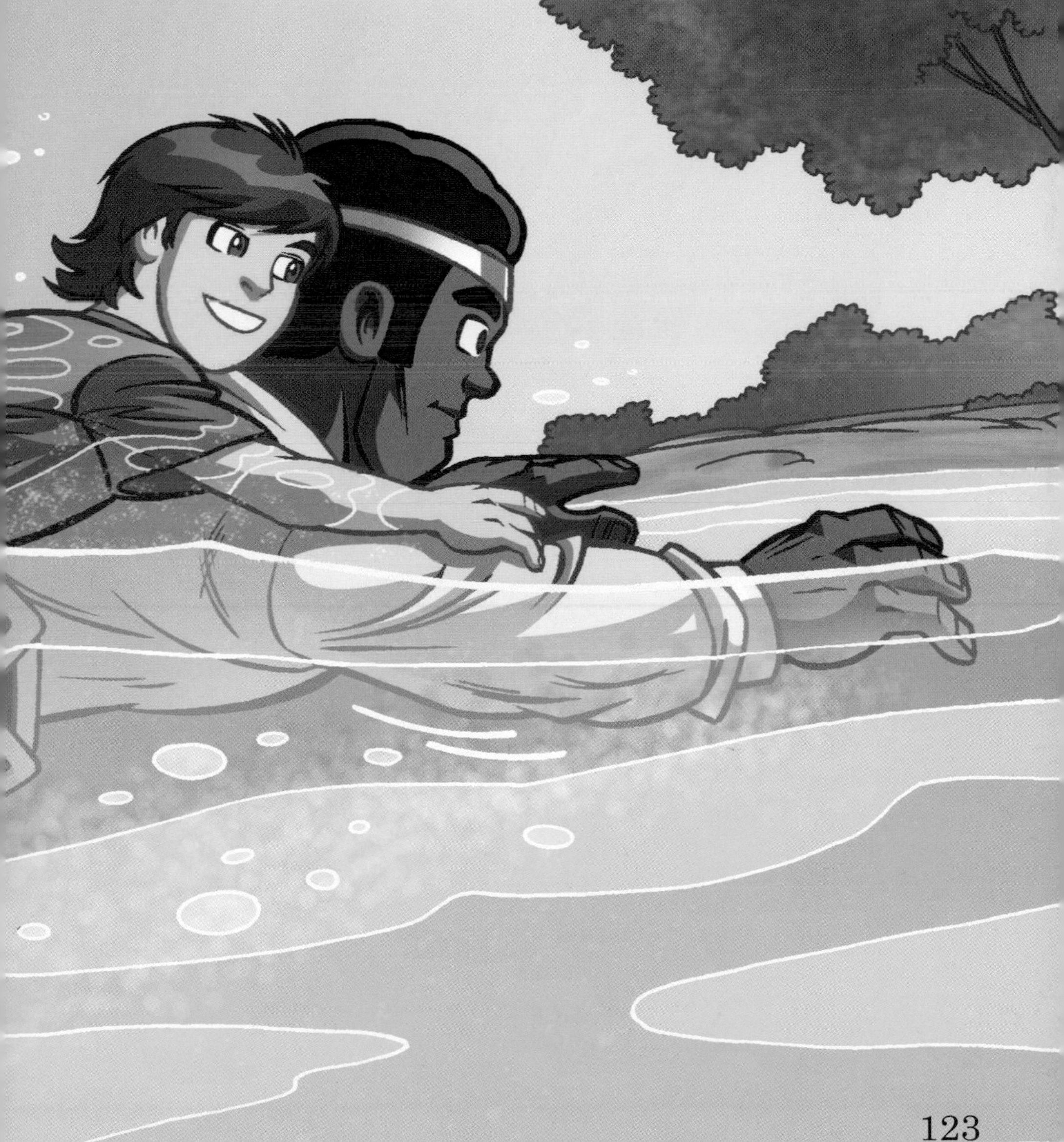

When Luke and the boy reach the riverbank, Juggernaut is already there.

"Looks like you are not the strongest guy around after all," Juggernaut smirks. "I win the contest!"

Luke Cage does not mind.
"You might be the winner," he says,
"but I feel like a hero!"

by Lucy Rosen
illustrated by Dario Brizuela
inks by Andres Ponce • coloring by Franco Riesco

LITTLE, BROWN AND COMPANY
New York   Boston

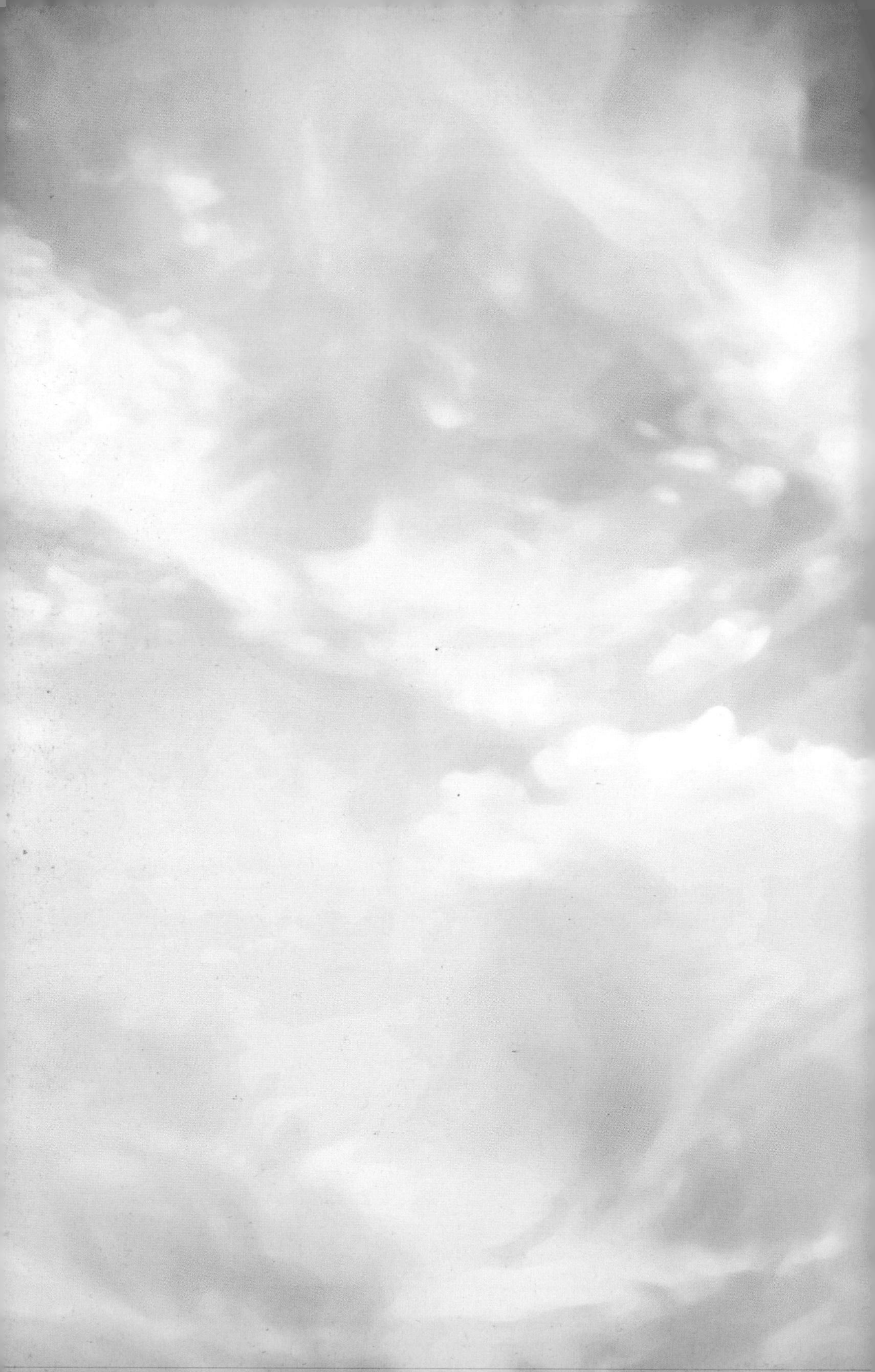

Attention,
all Super Hero Squad fans!
Look for these items when you read this story.
Can you spot them all?

DIAMOND

NECKLACE

MONKEY

PRAIRIE DOG

It is a quiet day
in Super Hero City.
Spider-Man, Ant-Man, and Wasp
are bored.

They walk by a jewelry store.

"Let us go in," says Wasp.

"I want to look at necklaces."

Spider-Man and Ant-Man shrug.

They follow her in.

"I need a necklace to match an outfit that I made," she tells her friends.

"Oh yeah?" snarls a nasty voice.
It is MODOK!
He and Enchantress
are robbing the store!

The heroes lunge at the villains, but Enchantress yells, "Freeze!" She uses mind control to stop them in their tracks.

"Let us scram," Enchantress says. She jumps into MODOK's flying chair as he blasts a hole through the wall.

Ant-Man, Wasp, and Spider-Man
snap out of their daze.
"Give those back," says Spider-Man.
He shoots a web at MODOK's chair.

ZOO

"As you wish," laughs MODOK.
He drops the jewels
as he and Enchantress zoom off.
The heroes cannot catch all of them.

Back at headquarters,
Spider-Man explains what happened.
Iron Man looks at a scan of the area.

"Looks like the jewels fell into the zoo,"
says Iron Man.
"A ruby ring landed near the monkeys.
A necklace is in the birdhouse.
And a big diamond is in a prairie dog den.
We will have to get past the animals."

The heroes hurry to the zoo.
"I will take the monkeys,"
says Spider-Man.
"Wasp, you take the birds.
Ant-Man, you get the prairie dogs."

At the monkey house,

Spider-Man quickly sees the ring.

He reaches out, but a monkey grabs it!

"Quit monkeying around!"

yells Spider-Man.

Over at the birdhouse,

Wasp searches for the necklace.

"Oh no," she cries.

A bird is tucking it into the nest!

Ant-Man is also having trouble.
A prairie dog has the diamond,
but the animal dives into its hole!
"Get back here!" shouts Ant-Man.

"What are we going to do?" asks Wasp. "We cannot grab the jewels without the animals seeing us." "I have a tiny idea!" says Ant-Man.

"Hold tight, everybody," he says.
He uses his powers
to shrink them all down to bug size!
"See if the animals spy us now!"

Spider-Man rushes back to see
that the monkey still has the ring.
"Time to go bananas,"
jokes Spider-Man.

He spins a web so thin that
the monkey does not see it.
The animal swings right into it,
and Spider-Man grabs the ruby ring.

Back inside the birdhouse,

Wasp flies up to the nest.

She searches among the twigs.

"Got it!" cries Wasp
when she finds the necklace.
She jumps on the bird's back
to catch a flight down.
The bird never notices a thing!

Ant-Man jumps into the prairie dog hole.
The big, shiny diamond is in the den,
but Ant-Man is now too small to lift it!

"Care to lend some hands?"
he calls out to his friends.
Spider-Man and Wasp
help him carry out the diamond.

Ant-Man returns all three of them to normal size.

"We did it!" the heroes shout.

"Not exactly," growls a familiar voice.

Enchantress and MODOK are back!

"We want to keep the jewels after all," Enchantress says.
"How nice of you to get them for us." Ant-Man, Spider-Man, and Wasp know just what to do.

Ant-Man shrinks the other heroes again.

"What is going on here?"

asks MODOK in surprise.

Wasp buzzes around the bad guys.

"Stop that noise!" they cry.

Enchantress and MODOK

try to run away,

but Spider-Man traps them in a web!

"Nice job, guys," says Ant-Man. "Looks like teamwork comes in all sizes!"

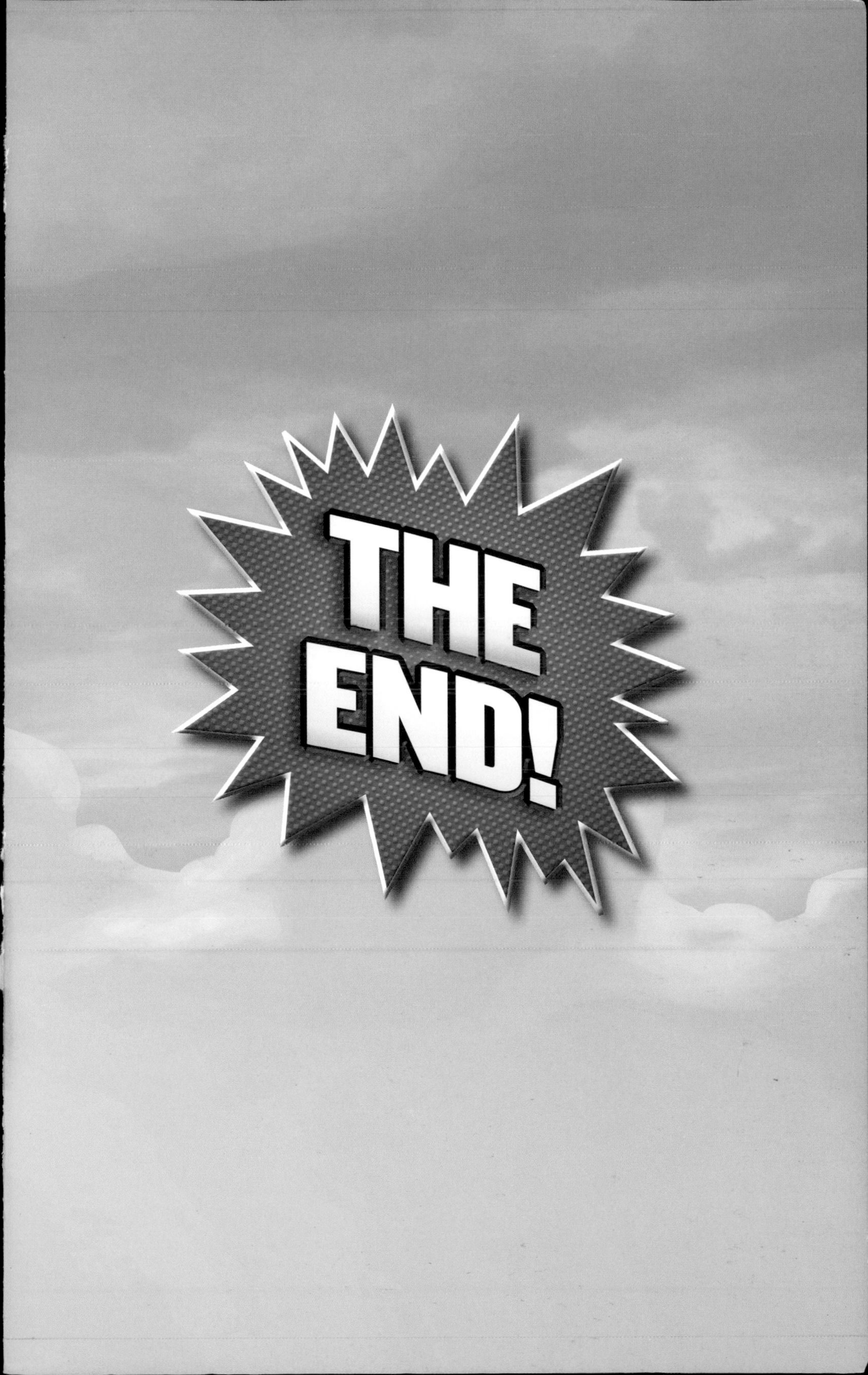
THE END!

Read more adventures of the

MARVEL SUPER HERO SQUAD

IRON MAN'S SUPER POWER MIX-UP

MARVEL SUPER HERO SQUAD

MAGNETO VERSUS WOLVERINE

MARVEL SUPER HERO SQUAD

CAPTAIN AMERICA DOOM'S DAY

FREE PUNCH-OUT MASK INSIDE!

MARVEL SUPER HERO SQUAD

HULK SAVES THE DAY!

MARVEL SUPER HERO SQUAD

DR. STRANGE VERSUS THE SENTINELS

INCLUDES REUSABLE STICKERS!

MARVEL SUPER HERO SQUAD

THOR'S BIG ADVENTURE

CHECKPOINTS IN THIS BOOK

TEAM SPIRIT!

WORD COUNT	GUIDED READING LEVEL	NUMBER OF DOLCH SIGHT WORDS
572	I	102

THE TROUBLE WITH THOR

WORD COUNT	GUIDED READING LEVEL	NUMBER OF DOLCH SIGHT WORDS
526	I	86

MEET THE VILLAINS OF VILLAINVILLE

WORD COUNT	GUIDED READING LEVEL	NUMBER OF DOLCH SIGHT WORDS
435	K	70

SUPER HERO SHOWDOWN!

WORD COUNT	GUIDED READING LEVEL	NUMBER OF DOLCH SIGHT WORDS
458	K	80

THE INCREDIBLE SHRINKING SQUAD!

WORD COUNT	GUIDED READING LEVEL	NUMBER OF DOLCH SIGHT WORDS
590	J	92